The Many Kinds of Hot

by Dale-Marie Bryan

amicus
readers

Ideas for Parents and Teachers

Amicus Readers let children practice reading informational texts at the earliest reading levels. Familiar words and concepts with close photo-text matches support early readers.

Before Reading

- Discuss the cover photo with the child. What does it tell him?
- Ask the child to predict what she will learn in the book.

Read the Book

- "Walk" through the book and look at the photos. Let the child ask questions.
- Read the book to the child, or have the child read independently.

After Reading

- Use the picture glossary at the end of the book to review the text.
- Prompt the child to make connections. Ask: What are other words for hot?

Amicus Readers are published by Amicus
P.O. Box 1329, Mankato, MN 56002
www.amicuspublishing.us

Library of Congress
Cataloging-in-Publication Data
Bryan, Dale-Marie, 1953-
  The many kinds of hot / Dale-Marie Bryan.
    pages cm. -- (So Many Synonyms)
  ISBN 978-1-60753-510-2 (hardcover) -- ISBN 978-1-60753-540-9 (eBook)
  1. English language--Synonyms and antonyms--Juvenile literature. I. Title.
  PE1591.B764 2013
  428.1--dc23
                    2013010405

Photo Credits: Shutterstock Images, cover, 1, 6, 7, 8, 9, 16 (middle left), 16 (bottom left); Sandra Cunningham/Shutterstock Images, 3; Vladis Chern/Shutterstock Images, 5, 16 (top left); Valentyn Volkov/Shutterstock Images, 10, 16 (top right); Phil McDonald/Shutterstock Images, 13, 16 (middle right); Jason Patrick Ross/Shutterstock Images, 14, 15, 16 (bottom right)

Produced for Amicus by The Peterson Publishing Company and Red Line Editorial.

Editor Jenna Gleisner
Designer Becky Daum
Printed in the United States of America
Mankato, MN
July, 2013
PA 1938
10 9 8 7 6 5 4 3 2 1

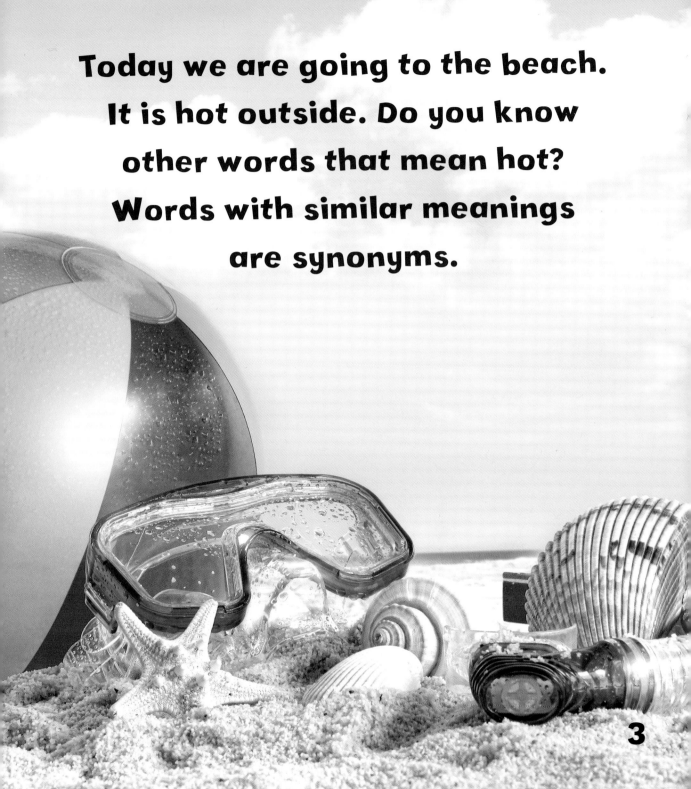

Today we are going to the beach. It is hot outside. Do you know other words that mean hot? Words with similar meanings are synonyms.

Sweltering means hot.

Today feels sweltering.
The temperature is high when the
red goes far up the thermometer.

4

5

Scorching means hot.

The sun is highest in the sky at noon. It feels scorching. We wear hats and put on sunscreen.

Blistering means hot.

We run fast across blistering hot sand. We watch out for crabs. Crabs burrow under the sand to keep warm.

Sizzling means hot.

We cook sizzling hotdogs on the grill. Grills can use coals or gas to heat up.

Toasty means hot.

We roast marshmallows until they are toasty. We put them on graham crackers with chocolate to make s'mores.

13

Blazing means hot.

The beach is cool at night.
We start a **blazing** fire with
sticks and paper.

Synonyms for Hot

sweltering
uncomfortably hot

sizzling
starting to fry

scorching
burning hot

toasty
really warm

blistering
so hot it could make blisters

blazing
burning